This book belongs to:

_____

Miller the Green Caterpillar

TO Gabrielle,

"Every once in a while YA gotta believe"

Written by Darrell House
Illustrated by Patti Argoff

Publication of "Miller" is proof enough for me that "if you believe and try hard enough," dreams really do come true. I want to dedicate the book to my wife, Bonnie; my daughters, Em and Jessie, who keep me young at heart; and to the rest of my family for their unfailing encouragement. To Marlene, Katy and my many friends at the Broward County, Florida Library who have been truly supportive and provided so many opportunities to share my stories, poems and music with those who matter most . . . kids.

Darrell House

River Road Press
Kimberling City, MO 65686
www.riverroadpress.net

Printed in Hong Kong

Miller, the green caterpillar,
dreamed that one day he would fly.

And he climbed every flower and sapling and
tree as he tried to get close to the sky.

He talked to all manner of creatures,
some crawlies and others that flew,
as he tried to discover the secret
that might allow him to fly too.

The ants and the beetles were no help at all.

Mosquitoes and flies laughed at him.
They said he had to climb higher,
then left Miller out on a limb.

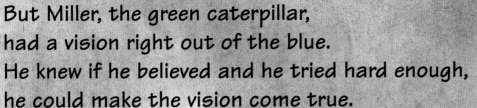

But Miller, the green caterpillar,
had a vision right out of the blue.
He knew if he believed and he tried hard enough,
he could make the vision come true.

He questioned his friends and his neighbors.
He asked everybody around,
if anyone knew how a green caterpillar
might get himself off of the ground.

His friend, Fred the frog, said, "Try jumping."

Greg, the grasshopper said, "Hop."

Miller tried everything he could think of
until he was too pooped to pop.

But then came a day in the autumn,
as rain was beginning to fall,
When the green caterpillar climbed under a leaf
to just get away from it all.

He tried to remember the things he had learned
as he huddled away high and dry.
But afraid that his dream might never come true,
Miller began to cry.

He wept all that night and next morning.
The teardrops kept falling 'til noon.

Then Miller, the green caterpillar,
began to weave a cocoon.

He didn't know what he was doing.
He didn't know why it was time.
But something was urging him onward;
a clock only he could hear chime.

All through the day he kept spinning away,
'til his shelter began to take form.
He finished the end and sealed himself in,
all safe and cuddly warm.

Tucked away in his comfy cocoon
Miller began to change.

And he had incredible, colorful dreams,
both wonderful and strange.

He had visions of wide-open spaces;
soft summer days without end.
He was flying as fast as an eagle,
rushing ahead of the wind.

The dream seemed to go on forever.
The changes were subtle and slow.
But at last came a day in the spring,
when it was time to get on with the show.

The sun was shining that morning,
right on Miller's cocoon.
A melody ran in and out of his head,
like an old familiar tune.

It sang of joy in the morning,
and wonderful things to come,
and Miller, the green caterpillar,
suddenly started to hum.

He stretched his legs and pushed so hard
the cocoon was ripped apart.
He crawled outside his broken shell
and the sunlight warmed his heart.

He filled his chest with clean, fresh air,
and suddenly, lo and behold.
Miller witnessed a miracle
as his wings began to unfold.

He moved them slowly up and down
until they felt just right.
Then Miller, no longer a green caterpillar,
lifted off in flight.

He floated over flowerbeds
and up among the trees.
Miller, the beautiful butterfly,
could go anywhere he pleased.

Tears came again to his newborn eyes
as he watched the world go by.

He had believed and tried hard enough,
and at last, he was learning to fly.

Believing in dreams and wishes
is not always easy, that's true.
But it worked for the green caterpillar

. . . it can certainly happen for you.